Geoffroy de Pennart

Sophie the Musical Cow

MYRIAD BOOKS LIMITED

MYRIAD BOOKS LIMITED
35 Bishopsthorpe Road, London SE26 4PA

First published in 1999 by Editions Kaleidoscope,
11 Rue de Sevres, 75006 Paris

ISBN 1 84746 062 3
EAN 978 1 84746 062 2

Printed in China

Sophie the cow lives in the country. She is very musical and loves to entertain her family and friends by playing the piano and singing.

One day a big musical competition was organised.

All the orchestras in the land were invited to take part.

"I think I'll try my luck," Sophie told her friends.

"I will try to find an orchestra that needs a singer."

"You want to go to the big city?" exclaimed her mother.

"You want to leave home?" cried her father.

"What about our evening concerts?" sobbed her friends.

"Listen," said George the old horse, "we're all a little worried.
But Sophie's right. She must give it a try. She has talent and she'll make it."

George persuaded everyone.

On the morning of her departure, everyone went with Sophie to the station....

....finally Sophie reached the big city!

Sophie bought a newspaper and a map, sat down
in the café and looked through the adverts.

Many orchestras were looking for musicians.

"Hmmm, let's see. This one,

The Grand Sparkly Smile Orchestra, is very near.

Strange name! Oh well, let's give it a try…"

"Are you here for the job? We don't usually hire grass-eaters, we're all meat-eaters here."

Sophie ran away as fast as she could.

"I'd better be more careful about the names of these orchestras," she thought.

"Ah, here's one for me. *The Music-Loving Grass-Eaters.*
I'm a grass-eater, let's give it a try…"

"Have you arrived for the position? Sorry my dear, you don't carry enough weight!"

"What does weight have to do with music?"
muttered Sophie.

"Hmm! Here's another. *Cud-chewers Royal Harmony.*
I chew my cud, so let's give it a try..."

"Are you here for the interview?
Sorry my dear. I'm afraid that you are not quite tall enough!"

"What does height have to do with music?"
grumbled Sophie.

"Here's another. *Horned Animals Music Circle*.

I've got a horn, so let's give it a try…"

"Are you here for the interview?
Sorry my dear. I'm afraid that there are horns and there are horns…"

"What do horns have to do with music?" thought Sophie.

"Hmm! Here's another. *Cows Orchestral Ensemble.*

I'm a cow. Let's give it a try…"

"Sorry. No brown cows in our orchestra!"

"What does colour have to do with music?"
muttered Sophie.

"Here we are. *Musical Bovines*.

I'm a bovine, so let's give it a try…"

"Are you here for the interview?
Sorry my dear. I'm afraid that you aren't quite elegant enough for our orchestra."

"What a bunch of snobs!" ranted Sophie.
"What does elegance have to do with music?"
She picked up her newspaper.
"Here. *The Grand Mad Cow Orchestra.*
I'm a cow and I'm as mad as can be.
Let's give it a try…"

"Are you here for the interview? Come in, come in, the more the merrier..."

"Eh, I think I've got the wrong address," stuttered Sophie.

Sophie was totally discouraged.

Royal Canine Orchestra. Purring Cat Orchestra.

No point in even trying...

"I guess it's time to go home."

Feeling sad, she sat down at the station café.

"Dear me, little lady, is anything wrong?" asked the waiter.

Sophie told him the whole story.

"Oh, I'm not surprised, little lady. All those orchestras are awful! I too am a musician,
and I've been through it all: my hair was either too long or not long enough, my ears hung down,
my nose was too pointy, I was too small or the wrong colour…"

"So," said Sophie, "why don't we start our own orchestra?
We could hire musicians on talent alone!
Let me introduce myself: I'm Sophie."
"Let's shake, little lady. I'm Douglas."
"Stop calling me 'little lady' Douglas, and we'll get along fine!"

Sophie and Douglas put an advert in the newspaper and there was a great response.